nature's friends

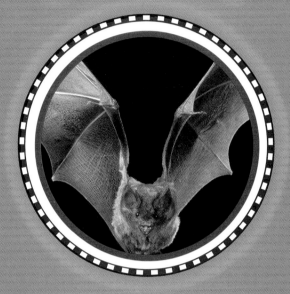

Bats

by Ann Heinrichs

Science Adviser: Terrence E. Young Jr., M.Ed., M.L.S., Jefferson Parish (La.) Public Schools
Content Adviser: Jan Jenner, Ph.D.
Reading Adviser: Dr. Linda D. Labbo, Department of Reading Education, College of Education, The University of Georgia

COMPASS POINT BOOKS
MINNEAPOLIS, MINNESOTA

Compass Point Books
3109 West 50th Street, #115
Minneapolis, MN 55410

Visit Compass Point Books on the Internet at *www.compasspointbooks.com*
or e-mail your request to *custserv@compasspointbooks.com*

Photographs ©: Tom Stack & Associates/Joe McDonald, cover, 11, 12–13; Bruce Coleman Inc./
Kim Taylor, 4–5, 6–7; W. Perry Conway/Corbis, 8–9; Visuals Unlimited/Rick and Nora Bowers, 15;
Bill Beatty, 16, 24–25; Unicorn Stock Photos/Tommy Dodson, 18–19; Photo Researchers/
Stephen Krasemann, 20–21; Bruce Coleman Inc./Jane Burton, 22–23; Digital Vision, 27.

Editor: Patricia Stockland
Photo Researcher: Marcie C. Spence
Designer: The Design Lab

Library of Congress Cataloging-in-Publication Data
Heinrichs, Ann.
  Bats / by Ann Heinrichs.
    p. cm. — (Nature's friends)
Summary: Describes different types of bats and their physical characteristics, methods of motion,
feeding habits, and life cycles.
Includes bibliographical references and index.
ISBN 0-7565-0591-7
1. Bats—Juvenile literature. [1. Bats.] I. Title. II. Series.
QL737.C5H46 2004
599.4—dc22   2003014437

Table of Contents

NOTE: In this book, words that are defined in the glossary are in **bold** *the first time they appear in the text.*

Creatures of the Night

Bats are creatures of the night. They sleep in dark places all day. Then they come out at night. They go sweeping and swooping through the sky.

Bats are full of mystery. People around the world are curious about bats. However, not many people understand them. Some people tell scary stories about bats. These tales make some people afraid of bats.

In China, bats stand for good luck, happiness, and long life. This idea is closer to the truth. Bats are great friends to humans. They eat tons of insects every night. Without bats, we could not play outside on summer nights. There would be too many mosquitoes! Let's meet our bat friends—and solve some mysteries, too.

◀ *A long-eared bat skims the top of a pond for insects.*

Flying Foxes and Flying Mice

Bats live almost everywhere. However, they do not live in very cold or hot regions or on some isolated islands. There are almost 1,000 **species,** or kinds, of bats. They belong to two simple groups—large bats and small bats.

Large bats are called flying foxes or fruit bats. They live in Africa, Australia, most of Asia, and some islands in the Pacific Ocean. They have long **snouts**—just like foxes! These bats eat fruit or suck **nectar** from flowers.

Small bats look a little like mice. The German word for bat is *fledermaus.* That means "flying mouse"!

Small bats have big ears. A small bat's snout looks like a pig's or bulldog's nose. Most small bats are insect eaters. A few tropical bats feed on the blood of birds, lizards, frogs, fish, or other animals.

Two fruit bats feed from blossoms. ▶

What Is a Bat?

Bats are small, fuzzy mammals. They can fly, but they are not birds. Birds have feathers and lay eggs. Bats have hair, like other mammals. Their babies are born live, not hatched from eggs, and are fed milk.

Some mammals can glide short distances. One example is the flying squirrel. However, bats are the only mammals that truly fly. They dive and dip and soar high in the sky.

The giant flying fox is one of the world's biggest bats. Its wings spread more than 5 feet (1.5 meters). The hog-nosed bat is one of the world's smallest bats. It is also called the bumblebee bat. Its body is only about 1 inch (3 centimeters) long. The Philippine bamboo bat has a **wingspan** of barely 6 inches (15 cm). Each of these bats weighs less than a penny!

◄ *A flying fox shows its huge wingspan while hanging in a cage.*

A Bat's Body

Bats are covered with silky fur. It might be brown, gray, black, white, or even red or yellow. The fur color helps bats blend in with their surroundings.

Bats are built much like other mammals. They are **warm-blooded.** They have a brain and a heart. They have eyes, ears, and a nose. Their mouths have teeth and a tongue. Bats have a good sense of smell. Mother bats often find their babies by smell.

Bats have four legs. The front legs are their wings! The back legs are short. If bats walk, they can be very clumsy. Some bats have short tails. Others have long tails, like mice.

Bats are very clean animals. Like cats, they **groom** themselves every day. They carefully clean their fur and wings.

A bat uses its front legs as wings. They have fur on these wings, but it is usually too fine to see. ▶

How Do Bats Fly?

Scientists call the bat **order** Chiroptera. That word is Greek for "hand-wing." A bat's wings, or front legs, are really its arms and hands.

Bats have a thumb and four fingers—just like you. Their fingers are very long. Sheets of skin stretch between the fingers. This skin also connects to the body. The wing skin feels like soft, thin leather.

On top of each wing is the thumb. It is a little claw. The back feet have claws, too. Bats cling to walls and trees with their claws. They also climb with their claws.

When flying, bats don't flap their wings like birds. Bats use their chest and back muscles, pulling their arms up, around, and over. They move like a swimmer doing the butterfly stroke!

◀ *Bats use their thumbs to climb, eat, and fight. These thumbs are on the top edge of their wings.*

What Big Ears You Have!

Sometimes people say "blind as a bat." Bats are not blind at all, though. They just use their hearing more than their sight. Some bats have enormous ears!

Bats find tiny flying insects in the dark. How do they do that? Bats send out a high-pitched sound. Humans can barely hear this sound. The sound waves bump into an object. Then they bounce back to the bat's ears as an echo. Bats use these echoes to help them find things, even their babies. Scientists call this echolocation.

Bats can tell a lot from that echo. They learn where the object is. They learn how large it is. They can even tell which way the object is moving. They do all of this in complete darkness. Bats use echolocation to "see" in the dark.

The California leaf-nosed bat has very large ears.
They help the bat find food and other objects. ▶

Life as a Bat

Many bats live in **colonies,** or groups. Millions of bats may live in one colony! They **roost** in caves, hollow trees, or empty buildings.

A baby bat is called a pup. Most female bats have one pup a year. The pup feeds on its mother's milk. Some pups hang on to their mother when she flies. Others stay home. They may play together and tumble around on the ground.

Bat pups grow quickly. Most bats reach adult size in about two months. They may live more than 30 years.

Some bat species hibernate in the winter. They go into a deep sleep. Some species **migrate** before winter comes. They travel to a warmer place.

◀ *A little brown bat pup clings to a tree.*

Hanging Around
All Day

While most other animals are going to sleep, bats are waking up. They spend the night hunting for food.

Daytime is quite another story. Bats sleep in the daytime. They roost in a sheltered place, far from light and noise.

Bats hang upside down when they sleep. They fold their wings close to their bodies. They grip with their claws. Then they can let go and take off quickly if they have to.

The body heat in most bats drops while they sleep. Lower body heat helps bats save energy for the big night ahead.

A colony of bats in Goa Lawah, Bali, Indonesia ▶

Life in a Bat Colony

If you were a bat, you would probably want to live in a bat colony. Bats feel safe in a colony. They keep each other warm, too.

Bats take care of their colony mates. Mother bats also help feed other bats' babies.

Some famous bat colonies live in Texas. These bats are Mexican free-tailed bats. One colony roosts in Bracken Cave near San Antonio. It's made up of more than 20 million bats! Another colony roosts under a bridge in Austin. More than 1 million bats swoop out together on summer evenings. Tourists come from miles around to watch them!

◀ *Many people visit Bracken Cave in Texas to see millions of Mexican free-tailed bats come out at night.*

Are Bats Dangerous?

Some people are afraid of bats. They have heard stories about bats biting or sucking blood. However, only three species of bats feed on blood. Vampire bats are the best known. They live in South America, Central America, and parts of Mexico.

Vampire bats do not like human blood. They prefer the blood of large animals such as cattle, horses, pigs, and large birds. They cut an animal's skin with their razor-sharp teeth. Then they lick the trickle of blood.

A bat may bite someone if it is afraid. Bat bites are like squirrel bites. Any wild animal bite may carry a disease. You should see a doctor for these bites.

A vampire bat ▶

What If I Find a Bat?

You may find a bat on the ground. It could be lost or sick or just worn out. It might be a pup that has lost its mother.

If you find a bat, do not touch it. Call an adult who can get help. Most cities have an animal rescue society. Its workers know how to handle bats safely. They will take the bat to a new home. It may need medical care. It may only need to get back to familiar surroundings.

What if a bat flies into your house? Just open a window or door. Then turn off the lights. It will fly outside.

◀ *A rescue worker holds a little brown bat pup. Remember, only trained adults should hold bats.*

Bats Are Our Friends

Without bats, we would be in big trouble! We would have too many insects. Some bats eat up to half their weight in insects every night. That's like you eating 30 pizzas!

Fruit- and nectar-eating bats spread **pollen** from one flower to another. Then the plants can make seeds and reproduce. Bat droppings, or guano, make good **fertilizer.** Bat droppings spread seeds, too. They help keep rain forests growing by spreading the seeds of tropical plants.

What's the biggest danger to bats? People! Many people do not understand these helpful animals. They destroy bats and their colonies. You can help by spreading facts about bats. You can build a bat house outdoors. Then you can watch how our bat friends live.

Red flying foxes are our friends. ▶

Glossary

colonies—places where groups of people or animals live together

fertilizer—a material that enriches the soil

groom—to clean and care for the body

migrate—to travel from one place to another at regular times

nectar—a sweet liquid matter that is produced by some plants

order—a category of animals in the scientific classification system

pollen—the tiny bits of dust from a plant that fertilize the seeds

roost—to perch or settle somewhere to rest

snouts—the long front part of animals' heads, which includes their nose, mouth, and jaw

species—a group of animals that can produce offspring with one another

warm-blooded—an animal that has the same body temperature no matter how its environment changes

wingspan—the length from the end of one wing to the end of the other when wings are spread out

Let's Look at Bats

Kingdom: Animalia
Phylum: Chordata
Class: Mammalia
Order: Chiroptera
Family: There are 17 families of bats.
Species: There are almost 1,000 species of bats. Forty-six species live in North America.

Range: Bats live all over the world except in extremely hot or cold regions and some isolated islands. They are especially abundant where the weather is warm and moist.

Life span: Most bats live 10 to 20 years. Some species live more than 30 years.

Life stages: Female bats are pregnant for 40 days to six months, depending on the species. Most females have one baby a year. It feeds on its mother's milk for several weeks. At about two months of age, it reaches adult size.

Food: Most bat species eat insects. Some species eat birds, lizards, frogs, or fish. Vampire bats feed on animals' blood. Flying foxes and fruit bats eat fruit or the nectar of flowers.

Did You Know?

The big brown bat has been clocked flying at 40 miles (64 kilometers) per hour.

The little brown bat is the longest-living mammal for its size. It can live more than 32 years.

The little brown bat can eat 600 insects an hour. The bats in Bracken Cave, Texas, eat more than 200 tons of insects every night.

Female vampire bats adopt orphan bats whose mothers have died.

Scientists are experimenting with vampire bat saliva to treat human heart diseases and strokes.

Bats make up nearly one-fourth of all mammal species in the world.

Junior Zoologists

Zoologists are scientists who study animals. You can be a zoologist, too. You will need a notebook, a pen or pencil, and some information about bats. Ask an adult to take you to the library or the zoo and help you find some information about bats. Then go on a Batty Safari! Find out about as many different kinds of bats as you can. In your notebook, write a description of each kind of bat you read about or saw. Write down what kind of food it eats and where it likes to live.

Now try to answer the following questions:

How many different kinds of bats did you find?

What things were the same about the bats?

What things were different?

How many of the bats that you saw eat insects? How many eat fruit or nectar? Did any of the bats you saw eat anything else?

What kinds of places do bats like to live?

Have you ever seen any bats near your home? If you have, where did you see them?

Draw a picture of a bat.

Want to Know More?

AT THE LIBRARY

Bash, Barbara. *Shadows of Night: The Hidden World of the Little Brown Bat.* San Francisco:
    Sierra Club Books for Children, 1993.

Earle, Ann, and Henry Cole (illustrator). *Zipping, Zapping, Zooming Bats.* New York:
    HarperCollins, 1995.

Greenway, Frank, and Jerry Young (photographer). *Amazing Bats.* New York: Knopf, 1991.

ON THE WEB

For more information on **bats,** use FactHound to track down
Web sites related to this book.

1. Go to *www.compasspointbooks.com/facthound*
2. Type in this book ID: **0756505917**
3. Click on the *Fetch It* button.

Your trusty FactHound will fetch the best Web sites for you!

THROUGH THE MAIL

Organization for Bat Conservation
39221 Woodward Ave.
P.O. Box 801
Bloomfield Hills, MI 48303
800/276-7074
For more information about how to help bats

ON THE ROAD

Eckert James River
Bat Cave Preserve
Southwest of Mason near State
Highway 290
Mason County, TX 76856
325/347-5758
To see millions of Mexican
free-tailed bats swarm from
their cave

Oregon Zoo
4001 S.W. Canyon Road
Portland, OR 97221
503/226-1561
To visit a zoo with bat exhibits

Index

About the Author: Ann Heinrichs grew up in Fort Smith, Arkansas. She began playing the piano at age three and thought she would grow up to be a pianist. Instead, she became a writer. She has written more than 100 books for children and young adults. Several of her books have won national awards. Ms. Heinrichs now lives in Chicago, Illinois. She enjoys martial arts and traveling to faraway countries.

W9-DAU-143

5-8